MARLEY'S CHAIN

Start Publishing PD LLC

Manufactured in the United States of America

Cover art: Shutterstock/Taisiya Kozorez

Cover design: Jennifer Do

10 9 8 7 6 5 4 3 2 1

ISBN 979-8-8809-0788-5

MARLEY'S CHAIN

by Alan E. Nourse

They saw Tam's shabby clothing and the small, weather-beaten bag he carried, and they ordered him aside from the flow of passengers, and checked his packet of passports and visas with extreme care. Then they ordered him to wait. Tam waited, a chilly apprehension rising in his throat. For fifteen minutes he watched them, helplessly.

Finally, the Spaceport was empty, and the huge liner from the outer Asteroid Rings was being lifted and rolled by the giant hooks and cranes back into its berth for drydock and repair, her curved, meteor-dented hull gleaming dully in the harsh arc lights. Tam watched the creaking cranes, and shivered in the cold night air, feeling hunger and dread gnawing at his stomach. There was none of the elation left, none of the great, expansive, soothing joy at returning to Earth after eight long years of hard work and bitterness. Only the cold, corroding uncertainty, the growing apprehension. Times had changed since that night back in '87—just how much he hardly dared to guess. All he knew was the rumors he had heard, the whispered tales, the frightened eyes and the scarred backs and faces. Tam hadn't believed them then, so remote from Earth. He had just laughed and told himself that the stories weren't true. And now they all welled back into his mind, tightening his throat and making him tremble—

"Hey, Sharkie. Come here."

Tam turned and walked slowly over to the customs official who held his papers. "Everything's in order," he said, half defiantly, looking up at the officer's impassive face. "There isn't any mistake."

"What were you doing in the Rings, Sharkie?" The officer's voice was sharp.

"Indenture. Working off my fare back home."

The officer peered into Tam's face, incredulously. "And you come back here?" He shook his head and turned to the other officer. "I knew these Sharkies were dumb, but I didn't think they were that dumb." He turned back to Tam, his eyes suspicious. "What do you think you're going to do now?"

Tam shrugged, uneasily. "Get a job," he said. "A man's got to eat."

The officers exchanged glances. "How long you been on the Rings?"

"Eight years." Tam looked up at him, anxiously. "Can I have my papers now?"

A cruel grin played over the officer's lips. "Sure," he said, handing back the packet of papers. "Happy job-hunting," he added sardonically. "But remember—the ship's going back to the Rings in a week. You can always sign yourself over for fare—"

"I know," said Tam, turning away sharply. "I know all about how that works." He tucked the papers carefully into a tattered breast pocket, hefted the bag wearily, and began trudging slowly across the cold concrete of the Port toward the street and the Underground. A wave of loneliness, almost overpowering in intensity, swept over him, a feeling of emptiness, bleak and hopeless. A chilly night wind swept through his unkempt blond hair as the automatics let him out into the street, and he saw the large dirty "New Denver Underground" sign with the arrow at the far side of the road. Off to the right, several miles across the high mountain plateau, the great capitol city loomed up, shining like a thousand twinkling stars in the clear cold air. Tam jingled his last few coins listlessly, and started for the downward ramp. Somewhere, down there, he could find a darkened corner, maybe even a bench, where the police wouldn't bother him for a couple of hours. Maybe after a little sleep, he'd find some courage, hidden away somewhere. Just enough to walk into an office and ask for a job.

That, he reflected wearily as he shuffled into the tunnel, would take a lot of courage—

*

The girl at the desk glanced up at him, indifferent, and turned her eyes back to the letter she was typing. Tam Peters continued to stand, awkwardly, his blond hair rumpled, little crow's-feet of weariness creeping from the corners of his eyes. Slowly he looked around the neat office, feeling a pang of shame at his shabby clothes. He should at least have found some way to shave, he thought, some way to take some of the rumple from his trouser legs. He looked back at the receptionist, and coughed, lightly.

She finished her letter at a leisurely pace, and finally looked up at him, her eyes cold. "Well?"

"I read your ad. I'm looking for a job. I'd like to speak to Mr. Randall."

The girl's eyes narrowed, and she took him in in a rapid, sweeping glance, his high, pale forehead, the shock of mud-blond hair, the thin, sensitive face with the exaggerated lines of approaching middle age, the slightly misty blue eyes. It seemed to Tam that she stared for a full minute, and he shifted uneasily, trying to meet the cold inspection, and failing, finally settling his eyes on her prim, neatly manicured fingers. Her lip curled very slightly. "Mr. Randall can't see you today. He's busy. Try again tomorrow." She turned back to typing.

A flat wave of defeat sprang up in his chest. "The ad said to apply today. The earlier the better."

She sniffed indifferently, and pulled a long white sheet from the desk. "Have you filled out an application?"

"No."

"You can't see Mr. Randall without filling out an application." She pointed to a small table across the room, and he felt her eyes on his back as he shuffled over and sat down.

He began filling out the application with great care, making the printing as neat as he could with the old-style vacuum pen provided. Name, age, sex, race, nationality, planet where born, pre-Revolt experience, post-Revolt experience, preference—try as he would, Tam couldn't keep the ancient pen from leaking, making an unsightly blot near the center of the form. Finally he finished, and handed the paper back to the girl at the desk. Then he sat back and waited.

Another man came in, filled out a form, and waited, too, shooting Tam a black look across the room. In a few moments the girl turned to the man. "Robert Stover?"

"Yuh," said the man, lumbering to his feet. "That's me."

"Mr. Randall will see you now."

The man walked heavily across the room, disappeared into the back office. Tam eyed the clock uneasily, still waiting.

A garish picture on the wall caught his eyes, a large, very poor oil portrait of a very stout, graying man dressed in a ridiculous green suit with a little white turban-like affair on the top of his head. Underneath was a little brass plaque with words Tam could barely make out:

Abraham L. Ferrel
(1947-1986)
Founder and First President Marsport Mines, Incorporated
"Unto such men as these, we look to leadership."

Tam stared at the picture, his lip curling slightly. He glanced anxiously at the clock as another man was admitted to the small back office.

Then another man. Anger began creeping into Tam's face, and he fought to keep the scowl away, to keep from showing his concern. The hands of the clock crept around, then around again. It was almost noon. Not a very new dodge, Tam thought coldly. Not very new at all. Finally the small cold flame of anger got the better of him, and he rose and walked over to the desk. "I'm still here," he said patiently. "I'd like to see Mr. Randall."

The girl stared at him indignantly, and flipped an intercom switch. "That Peters application is still out here," she said brittlely. "Do you want to see him, or not?"

There was a moment of silence. Then the voice on the intercom grated, "Yes, I guess so. Send him in."

The office was smaller, immaculately neat. Two visiphone units hung on a switchboard at the man's elbow. Tam's eyes caught the familiar equipment, recognized the interplanetary power coils on one. Then he turned his eyes to the man behind the desk.

"Now, then, what are you after?" asked the man, settling his bulk down behind the desk, his eyes guarded, revealing a trace of boredom.

*

Tam was suddenly bitterly ashamed of his shabby appearance, the two-day stubble on his chin. He felt a dampness on his forehead, and tried to muster some of the old power and determination into his voice. "I need a job," he said. "I've had plenty of experience with radio-electronics and remote control power operations. I'd make a good mine-operator—"

"I can read," the man cut in sharply, gesturing toward the application form with the ink blot in the middle. "I read all about your experience. But I can't use you. There aren't any more openings."

Tam's ears went red. "But you're always advertising," he countered. "You don't have to worry about me working on Mars, either—I've worked on Mars before, and I can work six, seven hours, even, without a mask or equipment—"

The man's eyebrows raised slightly. "How very interesting," he said flatly. "The fact remains that there aren't any jobs open for you."

The cold, angry flame flared up in Tam's throat suddenly, forcing out the sense of futility and defeat. "Those other men," he said sharply. "I was here before them. That girl wouldn't let me in—"

Randall's eyes narrowed amusedly. "What a pity," he said sadly. "And just think, I hired every one of them—" His face suddenly hardened, and he sat forward, his eyes glinting coldly. "Get smart, Peters. I think Marsport Mines can somehow manage without you. You or any other Sharkie. The men just don't like to work with Sharkies."

Rage swelled up in Tam's chest, bitter futile rage, beating at his temples and driving away all thought of caution. "Look," he grated, bending over the desk threateningly. "I know the law of this system. There's a fair-employment act on the books. It says that men are to be hired by any company in order of application when they qualify equally in experience. I can prove my experience—"

Randall stood up, his face twisted contemptuously. "Get out of here," he snarled. "You've got nerve, you have, come crawling in here with your law! Where do you think you are?" His voice grated in the still air of the office. "We don't hire Sharkies, law or no law, get that? Now get out of here!"

Tam turned, his ears burning, and strode through the office, blindly, kicking open the door and almost running to the quiet air of the street outside. The girl at the desk yawned, and snickered, and went back to her typing with an unpleasant grin.

Tam walked the street, block after block, seething, futile rage swelling up and bubbling over, curses rising to his lips, clipped off with some last vestige of self-control. At last he turned into a small downtown bar and sank wearily onto a stool near the door. The anger was wearing down now to a sort of empty, hopeless weariness, dulling his senses, exaggerating the hunger in his stomach. He had expected it, he told himself, he had known what the answer would be—but he knew that he had hoped, against hope, against what he had known to be the facts; hoped desperately that maybe someone would listen. Oh, he knew the laws, all right, but he'd had plenty of time to see the courts in action. Unfair employment was almost impossible to make stick under any circumstances, but with the courts rigged the way they were these days—he sighed, and drew out one of his last credit-coins. "Beer," he muttered as the barkeep looked up.

The bartender scowled, his heavy-set face a picture of fashionable distaste. Carefully he filled every other order at the bar. Then he grudgingly set up a small beer, mostly foam, and flung some small-coin change down on the bar before Tam. Tam stared at the glass, the little proud flame of anger flaring slowly.

A fat man, sitting nearby, stared at him for a long moment, then took a long swill of beer from his glass. "'Smatter, Sharkie? Whyncha drink y'r beer 'n get t' hell out o' here?"

Tam stared fixedly at his glass, giving no indication of having heard a word.

The fat man stiffened a trifle, swung around to face him. "God-dam Sharkie's too good to talk to a guy," he snarled loudly. "Whassa-matter, Sharkie, ya deaf?"

Tarn's hand trembled as he reached for the beer, took a short swallow. Shrugging, he set the glass on the bar and got up from his stool. He walked out, feeling many eyes on his back.

He walked. Time became a blur to a mind beaten down by constant rebuff. He became conscious of great weariness of both mind and body. Instinct screamed for rest....

*

Tam sat up, shaking his head to clear it. He shivered from the chill of the park—the cruel pressure of the bench. He pulled up his collar and moved out into the street again.

There was one last chance. Cautiously his mind skirted the idea, picked it up, regarded it warily, then threw it down again. He had promised himself never to consider it, years before, in the hot, angry days of the Revolt. Even then he had had some inkling of the shape of things, and he had promised himself, bitterly, never to consider that last possibility. Still—

Another night in the cold out-of-doors could kill him. Suddenly he didn't care any more, didn't care about promises, or pride, or anything else. He turned into a public telephone booth, checked an address in the thick New Denver book—

He knew he looked frightful as he stepped onto the elevator, felt the cold eyes turn away from him in distaste. Once he might have been mortified, felt the deep shame creeping up his face, but he didn't care any longer. He just stared ahead at the moving panel, avoiding the cold eyes, until the fifth floor was called.

The office was halfway down the dark hallway. He saw the sign on the door, dimly: "United Continents Bureau of Employment", and down in small letters below, "Planetary Division, David G. Hawke."

Tarn felt the sinking feeling in his stomach, and opened the door apprehensively. It had been years since he had seen Dave, long years filled with violence and change. Those years could change men, too. Tam thought, fearfully; they could make even the greatest men change. He remembered, briefly, his promise to himself, made just after the Revolt, never to trade on past friendships, never to ask favors of those men he had known before, and befriended. With a wave of warmth, the memory of those old days broke through, those days when he had roomed with Dave Hawke, the long, probing talks, the confidences, the deep, rich knowledge that they had shared each others dreams and ideals, that they had stood side by side for a common cause, though they were such different men, from such very different worlds. Ideals had been cheap in those days, talk easy, but still, Tam knew that Dave had been sincere, a firm, stout friend. He had known, then, the sincerity in the big lad's quiet voice, felt the rebellious fire in his eyes. They had understood each other, then, deeply, sympathetically, in spite of the powerful barrier they sought to tear down—

The girl at the desk caught his eye, looked up from her work without smiling. "Yes?"

"My name is Tam Peters. I'd like to see Mr. Hawke." His voice was thin, reluctant, reflecting overtones of the icy chill in his chest. So much had happened since those long-dead days, so many things to make men change—

The girl was grinning, her face like a harsh mask. "You're wasting your time," she said, her voice brittle.

Anger flooded Tarn's face. "Listen," he hissed. "I didn't ask for your advice. I asked to see Dave Hawke. If you choose to announce me now, that's fine. If you don't see fit, then I'll go in without it. And you won't stop me—"

The girl stiffened, her eyes angry. "You'd better not get smart," she snapped, watching him warily. "There are police in the building. You'd better not try anything, or I'll call them!"

"That's enough Miss Jackson."

The girl turned to the man in the office door, her eyes disdainful.

The man stood in the doorway, a giant, with curly black hair above a high, intelligent forehead, dark brooding eyes gleaming like live coals in the sensitive face. Tam looked at him, and suddenly his knees would hardly support him, and his voice was a tight whisper—

"Dave!"

And then the huge man was gripping his hand, a strong arm around his thin shoulders, the dark, brooding eyes soft and smiling. "Tam, Tam—It's been so damned long, man—oh, it's good to see you, Tam. Why, the last I heard, you'd taken passage to the Rings—years ago—"

Weakly, Tam stumbled into the inner office, sank into a chair, his eyes overflowing, his mind a turmoil of joy and relief. The huge man slammed the door to the outer office and settled down behind the desk, sticking his feet over the edge, beaming. "Where have you *been*, Tam? You promised you'd look me up any time you came to New Denver, and I haven't seen you in a dozen years—" He fished in a lower drawer. "Drink?"

"No, no—thanks. I don't think I could handle a drink—" Tam sat back, gazing at the huge man, his throat tight. "You look bigger and better than ever, Dave."

*

Dave Hawke laughed, a deep bass laugh that seemed to start at the soles of his feet. "Couldn't very well look thin and wan," he said. He pushed a cigar box across the desk. "Here, light up. I'm on these exclusively these days—remember how you tried to get me to smoke them, back at the University? How you couldn't stand cigarettes?

Said they were for women, a man should smoke a good cigar. You finally converted me."

Tam grinned, suddenly feeling the warmth of the old friendship swelling Back. "Yes, I remember. You were smoking that rotten corncob, then, because old Prof Tenley smoked one that you could smell in the back of the room, and in those days the Prof could do no wrong—"

Dave Hawke grinned broadly, settled back in his chair as he lit the cigar. "Yes, I remember. Still got that corncob around somewhere—" he shook his head, his eyes dreamy. "Good old Prof Tenley! One in a million—there was an honest man, Tam. They don't have them like that in the colleges these days. Wonder what happened to the old goat?"

"He was killed," said Tam, softly. "Just after the war. Got caught in a Revolt riot, and he was shot down."

Dave looked at him, his eyes suddenly sad. "A lot of honest men went down in those riots, didn't they? That was the worst part of the Revolt. There wasn't any provision made for the honest men, the really good men." He stopped, and regarded Tam closely. "What's the trouble, Tam? If you'd been going to make a friendly call, you'd have done it years ago. You know this office has always been open to you—"

Tam stared at his shoe, carefully choosing his words, lining them up in his mind, a frown creasing his forehead. "I'll lay it on the line," he said in a low voice. "I'm in a spot. That passage to the Rings wasn't voluntary. I was shanghaied onto a freighter, and had to work for eight years without pay to get passage back. I'm broke, and I'm hungry, and I need to see a doctor—"

"Well, hell!" the big man exploded. "Why didn't you holler sooner? Look, Tam—we've been friends for a long time. You know better than to hesitate." He fished for his wallet. "Here, I can let you have as much as you need—couple hundred?"

"No, no—That's not what I'm getting at." Tam felt his face flush with embarrassment. "I need a job, Dave. I need one bad."

Dave sat back, and his feet came off the desk abruptly. He didn't look at Tam. "I see," he said softly. "A job—" He stared at the ceiling for a moment. "Tell you what," he said. "The government's opening a new uranium mine in a month or so—going to be a big project, they'll need lots of men—on Mercury—"

Tam's eyes fell, a lump growing in his throat. "Mercury," he repeated dully.

"Why, sure, Tam—good pay, chance for promotion."

"I'd be dead in six months on Mercury." Tam's eyes met Dave's, trying to conceal the pain. "You know that as well as I do, Dave—"

Dave looked away. "Oh, the docs don't know what they're talking about—"

"You know perfectly well that they do. I couldn't even stand Venus very long. I need a job on Mars, Dave—or on Earth."

"Yes," said Dave Hawke sadly, "I guess you're right." He looked straight at Tam, his eyes sorrowful. "The truth is, I can't help you. I'd like to, but I can't. There's nothing I can do."

Tam stared, the pain of disillusionment sweeping through him. "Nothing you can do!" he exploded. "But you're the *director* of this bureau! You know every job open on every one of the planets—"

"I know. And I have to help get them filled. But I can't make anyone hire, Tam. I can send applicants, and recommendations, until I'm blue in the face, but I can't make a company hire—" He paused, staring at Tam. "Oh, hell," he snarled, suddenly, his face darkening. "Let's face it, Tam. They won't hire you. Nobody will hire you. You're a Sharkie, and that's all there is to it, they aren't hiring Sharkies. And there's nothing I can do to make them."

Tam sat as if he had been struck, the color draining from his face. "But the law—Dave, you know there's a law. They *have* to hire us, if we apply first, and have the necessary qualifications."

The big man shrugged, uneasily. "Sure, there's a law, but who's going to enforce it?"

Tam looked at him, a desperate tightness in his throat. "*You* could enforce it. You could if you wanted to."

*

The big man stared at him for a moment, then dropped his eyes, looked down at the desk. Somehow this big body seemed smaller, less impressive. "I can't do it, Tam. I just can't."

"They'd have to listen to you!" Tam's face was eager. "You've got enough power to put it across—the court would *have* to stick to the law—"

"I can't do it." Dave drew nervously on his cigar, and the light in his eyes seemed duller, now. "If it were just me, I wouldn't hesitate a minute. But I've got a wife, a family. I can't jeopardize them—"

"Dave, you know it would be the right thing."

"Oh, the right thing be damned! I can't go out on a limb, I tell you. There's nothing I can do. I can let you have money, Tam, as much as you need—I could help you set up in business, maybe, or anything—but I can't stick my neck out like that."

Tam sat stiffly, coldness seeping down into his legs. Deep in his heart he had known that this was what he had dreaded, not the fear of rebuff, not the fear of being snubbed, unrecognized, turned out. That would have been nothing, compared to this change in the honest, forthright, fearless Dave Hawke he had once known. "What's happened, Dave? Back in the old days you would have leaped at such a chance. I would have—the shoe was on the other foot then. We talked, Dave, don't you remember how we talked? We were friends, you can't forget that. I *know* you, I *know* what you believe, what you think. How can you let yourself down?"

Dave Hawke's eyes avoided Tam's. "Times have changed. Those were the good old days, back when everybody was happy, almost. Everybody but me and a few others—at least, it looked that way to you. But those days are gone. They'll never come back. This is a reaction period, and the reaction is bitter. There isn't any place for fighters now, the world is just the way people want it, and nobody can change it. What do you expect me to do?" He stopped, his heavy face contorted, a line of perspiration on his forehead. "I hate it," he said finally, "but my hands are tied. I can't do anything. That's the way things are—"

"But *why?*" Tam Peters was standing, eyes blazing, staring down at the big man behind the desk, the bitterness of long, weary years tearing into his voice, almost blinding him. "*Why is that the way things are?* What have I done? Why do we have this mess, where a man isn't worth any more than the color of his skin—"

Dave Hawke slammed his fist on the desk, and his voice roared out in the close air of the office. "Because it was coming!" he bellowed. "It's been coming and now it's here—and there's nothing on God's earth can be done about it!"

Tam's jaw sagged, and he stared at the man behind the desk. "Dave—think what you're saying, Dave—"

"I know right well what I'm saying," Dave Hawke roared, his eyes burning bitterly. "Oh, you have no idea how long I've thought, the fight I've had with myself, the sacrifices I've had to make. You weren't born like I was, you weren't raised on the wrong side of the fence—well, there was an old, old Christmas story that I used to read. Years ago, before they burned the Sharkie books. It was about an evil man who went through life cheating people, hating and hurting people, and when he died, he found that every evil deed he had ever done had become a link in a heavy iron chain, tied and shackled to his waist. And he wore that chain he had built up, and he had to drag it, and drag it, from one eternity to the next—his name was Marley, remember?"

"Dave, you're not making sense—"

"Oh, yes, all kinds of sense. Because you Sharkies have a chain, too. You started forging it around your ankles back in the classical Middle Ages of Earth. Year by year you built it up, link by link, built it stronger, heavier. You could have stopped it any time you chose, but you didn't ever think of that. You spread over the world, building up your chain, assuming that things would always be just the way they were, just the way you wanted them to be."

The big man stopped, breathing heavily, a sudden sadness creeping into his eyes, his voice taking on a softer tone. "You were such fools," he said softly. "You waxed and grew strong, and clever, and confident, and the more power you had, the more you wanted. You fought wars, and then bigger and better wars, until you couldn't be satisfied with gunpowder and TNT any longer. And finally you divided your world into two armed camps, and brought Fury out of her box, fought with the power of the atoms themselves, you clever Sharkies—and when the dust settled, and cooled off, there weren't very many of you left. Lots of us—it was your war, remember—but not very many of you. Of course there was a Revolt then, and all the boxed up, driven in hatred and bloodshed boiled up and over, and you Sharkies at long last got your chain tied right around your waists. You were a long, long time building it, and now you can wear it—"

*

Tam's face was chalky. "Dave—there were some of us—you know there were many of us that hated it as much as you did, before the Revolt. Some of us fought, some of us at least tried—"

The big man nodded his head, bitterly. "You thought you tried, sure. It was the noble thing to do, the romantic thing, the *good* thing to do. But you didn't really believe it. I know—I thought there was some hope, back then, some chance to straighten things out without a Revolt. For a long time I thought that you, and those like you, really meant all you were saying, I thought somehow we could find an equal footing, an end to the hatred and bitterness. But there wasn't any end, and you never really thought there ever would be. That made it so safe—it would never succeed, so when things were quiet it was a nice idea to toy around with, this equality for all, a noble project that couldn't possibly succeed. But when things got hot, it was a different matter." He stared at Tam, his dark eyes brooding. "Oh, it wasn't just you, Tam. You were my best friend, even though it was a hopeless, futile friendship. You tried, you did the best you could, I know. But it *just wasn't true*, Tam. When it came to the pinch, to a real jam, you would have been just like the rest, basically. It was built up in you, drummed into you, until no amount of fighting could ever scour it out—"

Dave Hawke stood up, walked over to the window, staring out across the great city. Tam watched him, the blood roaring in his ears, hardly able to believe what he had heard from the big man, fighting to keep his mind from sinking into total confusion. Somewhere a voice deep within him seemed to be struggling through with confirmation, telling him that Dave Hawke was right, that he never really *had* believed. Suddenly Dave turned to him, his dark eyes intense. "Look, Tam," he said, quickly, urgently. "There are jobs you can get. Go to Mercury for a while, work the mines—not long, just for a while, out there in the sun—then you can come back—"

Tam's ears burned, fierce anger suddenly bursting in his mind, a feeling of loathing. "Never," he snapped. "I know what you mean. I don't do things that way. That's a coward's way, and by God, I'm no coward!"

"But it would be so easy, Tam—" Dave's eyes were pleading now. "Please—"

Tam's eyes glinted. "No dice. I've got a better idea. There's one thing I can do. It's not very nice, but at least it's honest, and square. I'm hungry. There's one place where I can get food. Even Sharkies get food there. And a bed to sleep in, and books to read—maybe even some Sharkie books, and maybe some paper to write on—" He stared at the big man, oddly, his pale eyes feverish. "Yes, yes, there's one place I can go, and get plenty to eat, and get away from this eternal rottenness—"

Dave looked up at him, his eyes suspicious. "Where do you mean?"

"Prison," said Tam Peters.

"Oh, now see here—let's not be ridiculous—"

"Not so ridiculous," snapped Tam, his eyes brighter. "I figured it all out, before I came up here. I knew what you were going to say. Sure, go to Mercury, Tam, work in the mines a while—well, I can't do it that way. And there's only one other answer."

"But, Tam—"

"Oh, it wouldn't take much. You know how the courts handle Sharkies. Just a small offense, to get me a few years, then a couple of attempts to break out, and I'd be in for life. I'm a Sharkie, remember. People don't waste time with us."

"Tam, you're talking nonsense. Good Lord, man, you'd have no freedom, no life—"

"What freedom do I have now?" Tam snarled, his voice growing wild. "Freedom to starve? Freedom to crawl on my hands and knees for a little bit of food? I don't want that kind of freedom." His eyes grew shrewd, shifted slyly to Dave Hawke's broad face. "Just a simple charge," he said slowly. "Like assault, for instance. Criminal assault—it has an ugly sound, doesn't it, Dave? That should give me ten years—" his fist clenched at his side. "Yes, criminal assault is just what ought to do the trick—"

The big man tried to dodge, but Tam was too quick. His fist caught Dave in the chest, and Tam was on him like a fury, kicking, scratching, snarling, pounding. Dave choked and cried out, "Tam, for God's sake stop—" A blow caught him in the mouth, choking off his words as Tam fought, all the hate and bitterness of long weary years translated into scratching, swearing desperation. Dave pushed him off, like a bear trying to disentangle a maddened dog from his fur, but Tam was back at him, fighting harder. The door opened, and Miss Jackson's frightened face appeared briefly, then vanished. Finally Dave lifted a heavy fist, drove it hard into Tam's stomach, then sadly lifted the choking, gasping man to the floor.

The police came in, seconds later, clubs drawn, eyes wide. They dragged Tam out, one on each arm. Dave sank back, his eyes filling, a sickness growing in the pit of his stomach. In court, a Sharkie would draw the maximum sentence, without leniency. Ten years in prison—Dave leaned forward, his face in his hands, tears running down his black cheeks, sobs shaking his broad, heavy shoulders. "Why wouldn't he listen? Why couldn't he have gone to Mercury? Only a few months, not long enough to hurt him. Why couldn't he have gone, and worked out in the sun, got that hot sun down on his hands and face—not for long, just for a little while. Two or three months, and he'd have been dark enough to pass—"

www.ingramcontent.com/pod-product-compliance
Lightning Source LLC
Chambersburg PA
CBHW030416310726
48979CB00002B/443

* 9 7 9 8 8 8 0 9 0 7 8 8 5 *